Why My Dad?

A Story About Military Deployment

Written by Lisa R. Bottorff
Illustrated by Nicolas Peruzzo

D1295491

ISBN 978-1-61225-235-3

Published by Mirror Publishing
Milwaukee, WI 53214

Printed in the USA.

This book is dedicated to my nephew, Sean and my niece, Megan, whose father was a career U.S. Air Force Service Member, who spent many birthdays, holidays and school events away from his family, serving his country.

Michael and Randy have been best friends since Michael's Dad was transferred to the Post. They are always together. They are in the same class at school, played on the same baseball team and are in Boy Scouts together. Almost every weekend they slept over at one house or another. If you saw one, the other was always very close behind.

Every weekend during the summer they would camp out in Michael's back yard. It was tradition. His yard was big. It had a small pond, a large open field next door and backed up to woods. They had a small pup tent that was just the right size and would put it right on the bank of the pond.

They would play games, tell stories, play catch and run, run, run, until they both fell asleep. School was out. Spring was here and summer was fast approaching. The boys were excited about the summer ahead.

Michael's Dad was going to be the coach for their baseball team. The boys had already started practicing on their own. Randy could throw harder and farther. Michael could smash the cover off the baseball. They lost a lot of balls in the pond. Even if they would find one, it was too water logged to use again.

It was a Friday night, late in spring. The boys were dreaming of a great summer to come. They argued about baseball. They argued about who would bat clean-up and who would play which position. They talked about how they would spend the summer camping and staying up late. Soon that dream would be smashed.

Michael's dad was home early. When Michael saw his car, he ran in and grabbed his dad around the knees. He wouldn't let go. His dad was his idol. Michael told him they were ready for the season. "We don't need practice, Dad. We are ready!"

Michael's dad reached down and said, "Miks, we need to talk. You know that sometimes my job takes me away for a while."

Michael said, "I know Dad but you are always back soon. A couple of weeks at the most, right?"

Michael's dad looked into his son's eyes and tried really hard to smile but it just wasn't there. He said, "Well, Miks, this time I am afraid it will be a little longer than usual."

Michael looked at his dad; his dad was red in the face and close to tears.

"It will probably be at least October before I can come home. I have to leave right away. We can talk about it during dinner."

Michael yelled, "What about baseball?" and he ran from the house.

Michael came back a few hours later, his eyes beet red. His dad was gone. His mom was in the kitchen cleaning up. She said, "Miks, your dad wanted to talk to you and say goodbye but he couldn't find you. He waited as long as he could but he had to go so he wrote you this letter. He wants you to read it tonight in the tent after it is dark. I have a plate here for you if you are hungry."

Michael said, "I am not hungry. How long will he be gone this time?"

His mom answered, "I don't know, Miks. It's his job which he takes very seriously. He has lives to protect and sometimes he has to leave on a moment's notice to do it. He loves you very much. You know that."

Michael's eyes teared up. He took the letter and went to find Randy. Randy wasn't home so he headed for the tent. He grabbed his flashlight and slowly pulled out the letter. He sat there on a rock, staring at it. He couldn't open it. His eyes started to fill with tears. Just as he started to unfold the letter, Randy came in yelling, "The fireflies are here. They are everywhere!!! Grab your jar!"

Michael shoved the letter in his pocket. The boys grabbed their jars and flashlights and headed outside. They had been waiting all spring for the fireflies to return as this was the official start of summer. Baseball will soon follow.

They had found jars in Randy's pantry and poked holes in the lids for air. His Mom wouldn't miss a few of her canning jars. They headed toward the field next to Michael's house. Randy had already caught a bunch.

Randy yelled, "I have at least twenty. They are hard to count. What do you have Miks?" He turned around but Michael wasn't there. He looked around and saw Michael sitting on a stump, flashlight in hand, staring at a piece of paper.

Randy sat down next to Michael and asked, "What's that?"

Michael looked up with his eyes full of tears. He said, "My dad is gone. He left me this letter but I can't open it. Why is my dad always the one to leave?"

Randy had never seen his friend so upset. Randy really didn't know what to say.

He thought for a while and then said, "When my dad left, I felt the same thing. I know it is his job, but why can't he do it here? He told me that sometimes people do very bad things to others who cannot defend themselves. Sometimes it happens in an area far away. We have to help them."

Michael replied, "But why? Why do we have to help? Why does it have to be our dad's?'

Randy said, "My dad told me that sometimes people in power act like a bully. Remember when Tommy kept pushing me around? He'd shove me to the ground and make fun of me. He was a bully. I was too small and scared to defend myself. Remember?

"My brother Robbie stepped in and made the bully leave me alone. Robbie was big and strong and could easily stand up to him. Our dads are like Robbie. They are in the world's best military and they stand up to the bullies. Sometimes they have to go to other places to do it."

Michael replied, "I get it. They make the bullies back down. They help other people."

Randy smiled and said, "Right! That's their job. They go wherever they are needed. Sure I miss my dad too, but I know what he is doing is important and that helps to keep us all safe. They are all true heroes."

Randy grabbed his jar and headed out to catch more fireflies. He yelled back at Michael, "Come on. There are millions of them." Michael smiled and looked at this friend. Michael pulled out the letter from pocket. He slowly opened it. Through the tears he read,

"Miks, you are now the man at home. Knowing that you are here, taking care of your mom helps me more than you'll ever know. I will miss you both every minute I am gone. Knowing you are here helps me to concentrate on my job and keep everyone safe. I am proud of you. I love you and I'll see you soon."

Michael smiled as he knew his friend was right. He loved his dad and would miss him very much. But this was something his dad had to do and he was proud of him for it. Michael put the letter back in his pocket. He then pulled it out again and stared at it for a few minutes. He smiled, put it back in his pocket for another time.

Now, it was time to catch the most fireflies. He grabbed his jar and headed to find Randy; to find his best friend.

CPSIA information can be obtained at www.ICGtesting.com
Printed in the USA
LVIW01n2112290517
536235LV00002B/21